THE WAY IT HAPPENED

As Told in Words and Pictures by
Deborah Zemke

Houghton Mifflin Company
Boston   1988

For Sarah, Max, Mike, and my father,
a famous sea captain

Library of Congress Cataloging-in-Publication Data

Zemke, Deborah.
  The way it happened/as told in words and pictures by Deborah
Zemke.
    p. cm.
    Summary: The story of Sarah's fall from her bicycle changes with
humorous results as it is relayed from person to person.
    ISBN 0-395-47984-3 : $13.95
    [1. Humorous stories.] I. Title.
PZ7.Z425Way   1988   88-14742
[E]—dc19   CIP
                              AC

Printed in the United States of America

Y   10 9 8 7 6 5 4 3 2 1

It all started one morning quite innocently,
when Sarah Malone ran into a tree.

She told her friend Bill
just what had happened.

Bill told his father,
a famous sea captain.

The captain told his mate.

The mate told the crew,

including an ensign named Barnacle Sue.

Sue told a newsman.

He told it on TV.

Everyone heard it at the Waldorf Bakery.

The baker's helper told his wife.

And she told Willy who told Wanda who

told Max

who told Mike.

Mike knew he didn't do
whatever was done,
but he didn't know
what to do except to

RUN!!!!!!!!

He hopped on his bike
and rode desperately,
down the street,
out of town,

and smack into a tree.